D0408485

MONSTER HIGH™

DIARIES

MONSTER HIGH™

DIARIES

CLEO DE NILE
AND THE CREEPERIFIC MUMMY MAKEOVER

By *Nessi Monstrata*

LB
LITTLE, BROWN AND COMPANY
New York Boston

Little, Brown and Company

Hachette Book Group
1290 Avenue of the Americas, New York, NY 10104
Visit us at lb-kids.com

Little, Brown and Company is a division of Hachette Book Group, Inc.
The Little, Brown name and logo are trademarks of Hachette Book Group, Inc.

The publisher is not responsible for websites (or their content)
that are not owned by the publisher.

First Edition: August 2016

ISBN 978-0-316-26636-9

10 9 8 7 6 5 4 3 2 1

RRD-C

Printed in the United States of America

Written Record of Cleo de Nile

I miss my mom.

It's hard for me to say that out loud. When you are a member of a very important royal family like I am, it is necessary to not show your vulnerable side. After all, the people only want a royal family that is poised and perfect. That is what Father always says. A princess should never reveal weakness—it makes you an easy target.

But since this written record is private (and no one would dare disobey my orders to MIND THEIR OWN BUSINESS!), I feel comfortable expressing myself. Even though Mother has been missing for such a long time, she is not forgotten. There is a lot I remember about her, so she is <u>always</u> with me in memory.

Years ago, when we were still living in ancient Egypt, Mother and I used to love curling up together on a chaise longue to watch boo-vies while Father and Nefera would play games. Mother and I were big fans of romantic comedies. Today that is still my favorite kind of boo-vie!

My love of fashion also comes from Mother. When she would get ready for a night out, Mother would always allow me to try on her gowns. There was one gown that was so _beautiful_, I can still picture it. It was made of the finest 24-karat gold threads. My mom looked totally creeperific in it. She promised that when I was grown enough to fit into it, I could have it if I still wanted it. Of course, I've owned hundreds of gorgeous gowns since then, but I never forgot that one, or how amazing my mom looked wearing it. The gown was carefully packed away and preserved, and we still have it. Like me, it's waiting for her to come home.

But one of my most cherished memories of my mother is from a time when I was a very small girl. My parents had been invited to a gold-and-white ball, and I was upset that I wasn't allowed to come along. Even though she had much to do to get ready, Mother pulled me into her closet, dressed me in her most glamorous gold wrappings, and danced around her closet with me. Then, just for fun, she taught me how to put on makeup—Mother could do a smoky-eye look better than anyone—and gave me a special pot of my very own lip stain to keep. She told me it was "my color." All these years later, that is still my favorite shade in my whole lipstick collection. Mother always knew best.

I often wonder where my mom has been all these years. Though I would never admit it aloud, it is sometimes hard to go through life not knowing where your mom is or how things might be different if she were around.

So many things have changed since I last spoke with her. I go to Monster High and am the captain of the fearleading squad. My ghoulfriends are very different now from who they were in Egypt. I'm sure she would be shocked to hear I fang out with vampires and werewolves! And then there's Deuce. . . . Would Mother approve of my having a nonroyal boyfriend? Father certainly doesn't approve of him, but I like to think that my mom would. The only thing that hasn't changed during our years apart is my lipstick color—wearing the special shade she selected for me makes me feel as if my mom is still looking out for me from afar.

Even though life is a whole lot different, and I have grown up a lot in the years since we all lived together in Egypt, I'm sure if we were to see each other again now, Mother and I would still be very much alike. Some things never change, right? But sometimes I worry I will never know.... Because after all these years of my mother's being gone, I'm beginning to give up hope she will ever return.

Cleo

P lease pass the grapes," Cleo de Nile said. She arched an eyebrow and glanced across the enormous marble dinner table at her older sister, Nefera. Cleo cleared her throat to get her sister's attention. When Nefera didn't look up from her own meal, Cleo cleared her throat again. "Ahem. The grapes?"

Nefera finally peered out from under her long, dark eyelashes and gave her sister a withering look. "Do you need some water, Cleo?" she asked in a faux-sweet voice. Nothing about Nefera was ever *actually* sweet. "Your throat sounds parched. Are your wrappings too tight?"

"My throat is fine," replied Cleo. "And my wrappings are perfect." Cleo, the daughter of a mummy and heir to a five-thousand-year-old Egyptian dynasty, prided herself on her ability to remain graceful under pressure, but her sister really got under her bandages sometimes. She could be such a pain! Nefera had been home on a school holiday for a few weeks, and Cleo was counting the days until she would leave again. Their home was always so much more peaceful when her sister was gone. It was also strangely quiet and often sort of lonely, but peaceful nonetheless. "But I am *still* waiting for the grapes."

Nefera delicately waved her hand in the direction of a bowl of plump green grapes. It was sitting right beside her plate at the table, but rather than passing the bowl herself, she clapped once to summon one of the family's servants. She ordered, "Seti, would you bring Cleo the grapes?"

The servant hustled forward and whisked the bowl of grapes off the table. He carried it around the enormous stone table and set it down in front of Cleo's place setting. "Thank you, Seti," said Cleo, smiling. "That will be all."

The servant bowed low, then backed away from her chair.

"How was your day, my daughters?" Ramses de Nile asked in a formal voice as he dabbed at the corners of his mouth with a napkin. The moment Cleo's father placed his napkin on the table, a servant rushed forward and folded it into an elaborate pyramid. Such were the perks of living the life of Egyptian royalty. No need to lift a finger or use a crumpled cloth napkin—there was always someone nearby to make sure the de Nile family led a very luxurious life.

"My day was golden," Cleo said. "We had a monstrously good fearleading squad practice after school. We've been working on this new dance, and most of the other ghouls on the squad seem to be figuring out the routine pretty quickly."

"I seriously doubt that," Nefera said, rolling her eyes.

"Excuse me?" Cleo snapped, her blue eyes flashing. She flicked her long, straight black-and-golden hair over her shoulder and glared at her sister.

"Girls," their father cautioned.

"I *said*, 'I seriously doubt that.'" Nefera smiled, ignoring their father's warning. "The Monster High fearleading squad totally came unwrapped after I left. Your ghoulfriend Frankie Stein is always falling apart under pressure, and

Draculaura seems so distracted by Clawd Wolf that she never gets any of her steps right."

Cleo narrowed her eyes. Nefera had been the captain of the fearleading squad before Cleo took over, and the debate over who made a better team leader was a source of constant competition between the two girls. Nefera believed Cleo could never live up to her legacy. But Cleo knew the squad was better than ever with her as captain—in part because the current squad was made up almost entirely of ghouls who supported one another no matter what. Cleo would fight to the death to defend her ghoulfriends, and she knew the same could be said of the other ghouls on the squad. "How dare you say that about my ghoulfriends?!"

Nefera shrugged. "It's the truth."

"Girls—" Ramses de Nile warned. The girls' father ruled over the household with an iron fist.

He ran his life and family much as he had ruled his dynasty—his way or no way at all. And much of the time, it seemed to Cleo, he took Nefera's side. When they were young girls, Nefera had always been much more like their father, while Cleo had always been closer to their mother. When the girls' mother disappeared during the de Niles' escape from Egypt, things shifted a bit to make the family unit work without her. But still, Cleo always felt a little like the odd mummy out.

"What you just said is *not* the truth," Cleo said calmly but firmly. She didn't like to raise her voice to get her point across—a royal should never have to raise her voice to be heard. In a level, don't-mess-with-me tone, she added, "Frankie and Draculaura are both fangtastic dancers. They work very hard. And Clawd and Draculaura make an adorable couple. You shouldn't judge people, Nefera. And you definitely shouldn't say mean things about my friends. I won't stand for it."

"That is enough!" The ghouls' father slammed his fist on the table, making all the gold-encrusted platters and antique bowls rattle. Nefera and Cleo glared at each other across the table. Their argument was finally cut short when the door to the family's formal dining room flew open and the butler entered the room.

"Pardon the interruption," their butler said, bowing stiffly.

"What is it?" Ramses de Nile barked. He waved his hand, and a trio of servants rushed forward to clear the family's dirty dinner plates. As soon as the empty plates were gone, dessert dishes magically appeared before the three de Niles.

"A letter has arrived for you, sir," explained the butler. He held out a platter, on top of which sat an old-fashioned-looking letter. The paper was yellowed and dirty, and there was a wax stamp holding the parchment closed.

Ramses de Nile took the piece of mail off the plate gingerly. The letter looked fragile, as though it might crumble at the slightest touch.

Cleo took a small bite of her dessert while her father read through the letter. She watched his face go from confusion to concern to shock. "What is it?" she asked, putting down her spoon. A servant rushed forward to clear away the dirty spoon and replace it with a clean one for her next bite.

Her father took a deep breath. He looked up, gazing at each of his daughters with a vacant expression. "Father?" Cleo said quietly. "Are you okay?" Her father, who was usually very composed, looked as if he was coming unwrapped. It was very unlike him to show his emotions in such an obvious way.

Ramses de Nile took another deep breath before speaking. "I have something very import-ant to share with you," he said finally, his voice cracking.

Cleo and Nefera, who had been bickering only moments before, now shared a concerned look. *What's going on?* Nefera mouthed. Cleo shrugged back.

Finally, their father stood up. He crossed his arms and announced, "Girls, this letter is from your mother. She is coming home to us."

Written Record
of Cleo de Nile

For many years, I have wondered what happened to my mother when we were forced to flee our home after it was attacked. On that awful day, there was a great deal of confusion as we left our family home and dynasty. Father, Nefera, and I were hurried away from our palace to safety— while Mother, who had been in another wing of our home, was presumably led elsewhere.

In the months after our escape, I waited patiently for news about what had happened to my mom. We knew there was a good chance she'd been taken into hiding, just as the three of us had been. I had hoped she would rejoin us for the journey to the Boo World, but even after we arrived here, there continued to be no word. As more and more time passed, I began to really worry.

I don't know how to explain it, but I have always known deep down that my mom was okay. I've missed her <u>terribly</u>, and it worried me to not know what became of her, but I'd always felt in my heart that she was okay. So I'd held out hope for all these years that she would return to us in time. And that time <u>has finally</u> come! Oh. My. Ra!

After a lot of begging from Nefera and me, Father finally shared the details of her letter. There's still much we don't know, but here's what we did find out: When Father, Nefera, and I escaped, Mother was led to safety and instructed to hide out until the danger passed. She was promised that she would be reunited with all of us in just a short while. But a short while turned into a very long while, though we still don't know what prevented her from returning to us sooner. But I will find out soon enough!

I can't wait to see my glamorous, elegant mother again. I just know she's going to be exactly as I remember her. Finally, our family will be complete again!

Cleo

"Ghouls, I have *big* news," Cleo announced regally when she arrived in the Monster High Creepateria for lunch the next day. She waited until all her ghoulfriends' eyes were on her. Then she declared, "We have received a letter from my mother. She is returning home to us!"

"Are you totes *serious*?" Draculaura squealed happily, her eyes huge. The tiny vampire flashed her small fangs as she smiled, then she jumped up and squeezed Cleo into a friendly hug.

Cleo's smile widened. "Very serious," she said, taking her usual seat at the head of the lunch table. "She will be home soon"

Frankie Stein clapped and said, "Oh, Cleo, this is voltageous news! I can't wait to meet her." Suddenly, Frankie's hand popped off her arm. It scuttled across the lunch table and grabbed for one of Draculaura's french fries. Frankie—who had been built of spare parts in her father's lab—blushed a deeper green. She grabbed her hand and reattached it, then popped the fry into her mouth. "Whoopsie! Thanks for the fry, Draculaura."

"Don't mention it," Draculaura replied with a grin.

Cleo sighed contentedly as she looked at her ghoulfriends. Sharing her creeperific news with them made it feel even more special. But then she realized a couple of her closest ghoulfriends weren't there.

"Where are the other ghouls? I know they'll want to hear my big news right away."

"Lagoona has a swim-team meeting during lunch," Draculaura explained.

"And Clawdeen had to make up a test she missed last week because her morning track practice ran long," added Frankie.

Cleo was disappointed that all her best ghoulfriends weren't there for her big announcement. She sighed and said, "Oh well, I will tell them later, and I just know they will be so thrilled! Ghouls, you have *no* idea how glamorous my mom is. Her fashion sense is to *die* for, her hair is absolute perfection, and the parties she throws are talked about for centuries." She sighed dreamily, then paused dramatically before saying, "In fact, my father, sister, and I are planning a huge surprise party to welcome her home. We are going to throw a monstrously huge, fangulous ball! I'm sure Mother has gotten even more clawesome over the years—*I* certainly have, and I just know it runs in the family—so I bet her expectations for her welcome will be very high. I hope she will be pleased."

"Will *we* be invited to the ball too?" Draculaura asked, clearly excited about the chance to get dressed up.

"Will *I*?" asked Deuce Gorgon, sidling up behind Cleo. Deuce and Cleo were the golden couple of Monster High. They made a really cute pair, even though Deuce was totally low-key and relaxed, and Cleo was, well...not. He and Cleo balanced each other out. And together, they ruled the halls of Monster High.

Cleo grinned at Deuce. "Of course—you'll *all*

be invited. My mother will want to be introduced to all my friends, and I'm sure you're all just dying to meet her. Of course, you all know de Nile parties are absolutely legendary, so you won't want to miss it. I'm sure now that my mother has returned, parties at our palace will be even more incredible. She has the golden touch that will take everything to the next level."

"Sounds like this isn't gonna be my kind of party," Deuce mumbled. "Can I wear shorts?"

Cleo rolled her eyes. "Only the finest for my mom, Deuce. We'll get you a new suit. Obviously."

"So that's a *no* to shorts?" Deuce grumbled.

Cleo ignored him. "In fact, you'll all need new gowns." She turned her attention back to her ghoulfriends. "This is an occasion that will require the finest fabrics, the most fangtastic designs, extraordinary food...." Plans for her mother's welcome-home ball swirled around in Cleo's head. Thinking aloud, she whispered, "*Ooh,* maybe Clawdeen will help me design something one-of-a-kind to wear. I want to make sure my mother is impressed!"

"What if your mom has changed?" Draculaura asked suddenly. "I mean, what if she's lost her fashion sense or something?"

"How could something like that possibly happen?" Cleo asked loudly, her voice rising several octaves. She paused and cleared her throat. When she spoke again, her voice was soft and modulated again. "I'm sorry, Draculaura. I didn't mean to snap at you. It's just...absurd to think of my mother losing her fashion sense."

"Sorry, Cleo. You're right," Draculaura said. She and Frankie exchanged a worried look. Both ghouls hoped that Cleo's mom would be everything she remembered. But what if she wasn't?

Cleo and her friends spent the rest of lunch discussing outfits they could wear to the surprise party of the century. Then they talked about the food Cleo would have catered in and the decorations that would best welcome her mother to the Boo World. Deuce kept chiming in with party ideas of his own, and Cleo kept shooting them down because they weren't elegant enough. "Maybe you won't be invited after all," she said, after Deuce suggested changing the elegant Egyptian ball into a pool party, complete with waterslides and a lazy river. "This is a very serious event, Deuce."

Deuce chuckled. "Do you really think your mom's going to care what kind of party you have for this thing? Don't you think she's most interested in just seeing you and your fam again? Chillin', gettin' caught up, hangin' out…you know."

"This *thing*?" Cleo huffed, entirely missing the point of his question. "It's a *ball*, not a thing. And *chillin'*, Deuce?! You know my family doesn't *chill*. Ugh. This lunch is over." She stood up and spun around, preparing to storm out of the Creepateria—and away from Deuce—to make a point. But before she could get even halfway across the room, she heard Frankie shriek.

Sensing something was wrong, Cleo spun around. Frankie was crouched behind the ghouls' usual lunch table, her eyes the only thing Cleo could see peeking up over the edge of the table. Draculaura had already dashed away to meet up with Clawd before afternoon classes started. Cleo rushed back to the table, her face etched with concern. "Frankie?" she asked, tilting her head to one side. "Did you...*fall*?"

"Um," Frankie muttered. "Not exactly."

"Let me help you get up off the floor!" Cleo

said, reaching out to lend a hand to her friend. She was glad Frankie hadn't fallen but horrified by the thought that Frankie's adorable outfit was rubbing against all the screechza stains on the Creepateria floor.

Frankie smiled meekly. "I—I—" she began.

"You *what*?" Cleo said, urging her ghoulfriend to speak up. In her many years of life, Cleo had learned that you most often got what you needed when you asked for—or demanded—it.

Frankie bit her lip and said, "I, um, kind of ripped my skirt?"

"Let me see," Cleo ordered.

Frankie held up one corner of her skirt— an adorable, pleated black-and-white plaid—and grinned sheepishly. "It's bad."

Cleo put her hands on her hips as she surveyed the situation. "It *is* bad." Frankie's skirt had torn all the way up one side of her leg.

"I'll figure it out," Frankie said in a rush, tears filling her eyes. "No big deal. Once everyone leaves the Creepateria, I'll just sneak over to Headmistress Bloodgood's office. Maybe they have a spare skirt or pants I can borrow until the end of the school day."

"Oh my Ra, *no*," Cleo said, horrified. "You are *not* borrowing pants from the school office. Seriously, Frankie."

"Why not?"

Cleo began to laugh. "Total fashion disaster." She held out her hand again, urging Frankie to take it. "Come on," she said. "I'll sneak you out of here now, and we can try to do something to patch you up until the end of the day. I'm a pro at wrapping, so we should be able to figure something out to make this work for at least a few hours."

"Seriously, Cleo?" Frankie said as the warning bell rang. "You'll be late to class! And with everything you need to do to prepare for your mom's homecoming, and getting ready for the ball—you can't risk getting in trouble with the headmistress for being late to class."

"Don't worry about it," Cleo said, waving her off. "I never do anything I don't want to do. Now, come with me. Let's handle this fashion disaster in true de Nile style."

Written Record of Cleo de Nile

Preparations for my mother's surprise welcome-home ball are well under way. Father and Nefera and I have been working overtime telling our servants what to do to ensure that everything will be absolutely perfect. I can't believe she'll already be here tomorrow. I wish we could have the ball on her first night

home (what a way to be welcomed to the
Boo World!), but Father suggested we
wait until the weekend so more people
can attend. He also said we should
give her some time to adjust to her new
surroundings. That makes sense, but I hate
waiting.

It has been monstrously difficult
working with my sister on plans for the
event. She and I have very different tastes.
I am sure my choices are the right ones,
yet I have to fight with Nefera over every
single little detail. We've been disagreeing
about everything—the band, the food, the
colors of the custom-sewn drapes in the
ballroom, the shape of the ice cubes that
will be served with drinks . . . you name it,
we've discussed and disagreed about it!

Deuce keeps telling me none of this is very important in the grand scheme of things— that it's not the details of a party that are going to matter to Mother, it's the time she'll finally get to spend with us. But he's wrong. The party will <u>totally</u> matter. I'm not saying that material things and events are the only things that are important, but parties are essential! An elaborate welcome-home celebration is the perfect way to show Mother just how much we've missed her while she's been gone.

I'm sure Mother's standards for a royal ball will be even higher than either mine or Nefera's, so it's been pretty stressful preparing everything. This has to be the most special, most golden party in the history of parties!

There is one other thing I've been worrying about these past few days....

I almost don't even want to admit it, but here goes....

It is somewhat possible that my memories of Mother are a bit fuzzy. Of course, it's impossible to believe that I could be wrong about something, but it's been a really long time since Mother and I were together, and a lot has happened in the years she's been away.

I have a pretty clear recollection of many little moments with her, like when she would let me try on her jewels, but I'm not entirely sure all the details of my memories are totally accurate. I've heard that your mind remembers the things you want to remember but forgets the other stuff. It has been years since we've seen her, so what if I'm misremembering something important?

Or what if...like Draculaura said... what if she's changed? I guess I'll have to wait and see.

Cleo

CHAPTER THREE

el-*lo*!" A soft, melodic voice echoed through the halls of the de Nile palace. From her bedroom, Cleo could hear the gentle *click-clack* of footsteps in the front entryway. She glanced at the time—her mom wasn't due for two more hours, but it seemed that maybe she was early! De Niles generally prefer to be fashionably late, but Cleo was relieved her mother hadn't kept them waiting any longer. They had already been waiting decades too long to see her!

Cleo glanced in the mirror as she ran from her bedroom to greet her. What would her mother see when they finally came face-to-face again after all these years? What kinds of things would she ask her about, and would she be proud of the person Cleo had become? Would Cleo be fangtastic enough for her glamorous mother?

Dismissing her concerns, Cleo hustled through the palace to say hello. She raced through the upper levels, down the front stairs, and came to a stop near the front door. "Mother?" she called out.

"Cleo, darling," said a disheveled-looking woman standing beside Ramses de Nile. The woman was wearing a pair of too-short jeans and a faded T-shirt with a loose, button-up shirt over the top, and her hair was pulled back into a simple ponytail.

Cleo squinted. "Mother?"

"Oh, darling," the woman said. Her voice was becoming more familiar to Cleo. "It is so wonderful to see you again. I have missed you so much!" The woman stepped forward and pulled Cleo into a hug that felt strangely familiar. As Cleo let the woman pull her close, she tried to superimpose the memories of her mother on this... *stranger* who was in her house now.

Cleo's mother had been tall, just like this woman.

The newcomer had dark hair, just as Cleo's mother had. But Cleo remembered that her mother's hair had been long and silky, always styled in an elaborate braid with golden headbands and scarves.

The mother Cleo remembered was always wearing skirts and dresses, her clothing so weighted down with jewels and beads that Cleo had wondered sometimes how she hadn't fallen over during parties and dances. The woman standing before her now was wearing old *jeans* and a plain, button-up shirt!

"*Mother?*" Cleo whispered again as they looked each other over. "Is that...*you*?"

Cleo's mother laughed. "Yes, it is I. Much has changed since we last saw each other, Cleo. Let's get some snacks; we have much to catch up on!"

Ramses de Nile put his hand on his wife's arm. He too looked somewhat surprised—but also happier than Cleo had seen him in many years. Clearly, he could see past the wrinkled shirt and uncombed hair to the woman he had loved long ago. "You must be exhausted from your journey," he said, bowing slightly. "Wouldn't you like to take a bath and get changed while the servants prepare our dinner? We usually sit down to our meal at seven."

"Don't be silly, Ramses," she said, waving him off. "I'll just grab a snack from the kitchen. I don't want to waste another minute before we get to chat about everything that's happened over the years!" She laughed, a low, melodic sound that brought Cleo back hundreds of years.

"It *is* you," Cleo whispered, smiling at her mother.

"I am well aware that much about me has changed," Cleo's mother said with a smile. "But underneath my wrappings, I'm still very much the same mummy. Now, where is your sister? Let's find her, then we can get ourselves a snack and catch up on everything!"

❖　❖　❖

A short while later, Cleo, Nefera, and their father sat stiffly on the edge of settees and chaise longues in the formal living room, while their mom kicked her feet up and relaxed back into one of the chairs that were much more about fashion than function. She had prepared a snack of crackers, cheese, and grapes, laying everything out on a beautiful tray while the servants watched anxiously from one side of the kitchen.

"Madam," one of the servants had said nervously as Cleo's mother made her way around the enormous chef's kitchen. "Please, let us prepare something special for you. You should not be in here. This is our job."

"Nonsense," Cleo's mother said, waving him off. "Nothing special is necessary—I'm only digging up a snack! And I can certainly cut up my own cheese."

Nefera and Cleo had exchanged bewildered looks while they watched their mother get everything ready. Neither of the girls had *ever* cut a piece of cheese in their lives; they wouldn't even know where to find the cheese cutter. Their mother, on the other hand, seemed perfectly comfortable traipsing around the kitchen, pulling open drawers and cabinets to find things. She acted as if she had been in there a million times, and she seemed to have a knack for finding just what she was looking for. Cleo watched as her mother composed a delicious-looking snack without so much as one question as to where to find something or whom to call to come wash the grapes.

Now her mother was sitting in one of the chairs in the living room. It was a chair Cleo was pretty certain no one had ever sat in before. With her feet up and her arm slung casually over the arm of the chair, Dedyet de Nile actually looked *comfortable*. No one ever looked comfortable in the de Niles' formal living room. Their decorator had designed it to look good, not feel good.

"Do you know…" Cleo's mother looked around the room as she munched on a cracker topped with cheese (cheese and crackers was a rather *common* snack, but still, Cleo felt her stomach rumble as she watched her mother eat it). Dedyet pointed to a very ancient-looking vase etched with markings and to a bowl encrusted with jewels. "…that some of the relics in this room are one-of-a-kind?"

"But of course!" Ramses de Nile sputtered. As an antiques expert and a very rich man, Cleo's father prided himself on one-of-a-kind relics and treasures. "We would never showcase anything but the finest in our palace, my dear. Surely you remember the history behind some of these pieces? They have been in our family dynasty for centuries."

"We should consider loaning some of our most unique pieces to a museum," she said, gazing at a small figurine propped up on a bookcase. "It would be such a nice way to share our scaritage with other monsters."

Ramses de Nile's eyes widened. Before he could protest, Cleo spoke up. One of her favorite things about Monster High was that she got to meet all kinds of monsters and learn about so many different scaritages. If they loaned some of their family relics to a museum, it would be a wonderful way to share the most beautiful parts of their Egyptian scaritage with even more monsters in the Boo World. "I love that idea, Mother."

Cleo's mother smiled at her. "Cleo, darling, tell me about school. You must have many ghoulfriends? And are there...any mansters who have caught your eye?"

Cleo blushed. She wasn't ready to tell her mother about Deuce just yet. Cleo's father had never approved of her boyfriend, since his background was so different from the de Niles'. Ramses de Nile refused to give up hope that Cleo would someday marry into a family just as important as theirs. She couldn't seem to make him understand that for her, it wasn't about class or upbringing, but about the monster lurking underneath that. "First, we want to hear about you, Mother," Cleo said. "Please, tell us more of what happened after we were separated in Egypt. It must be such an exciting story—don't leave out one detail!"

Her mother sighed and stretched out like a sphinx. "There is so much to tell you. I don't even know where to begin."

"Might as well start from the beginning," said Nefera. "We have plenty of time."

"Well," Cleo's mother began, "while I was hiding out after the escape from our palace, I grew very bored and lonely. I was left alone for many weeks while the danger passed, and the only thing I had to fill my days were walls and walls of books. So I spent my days reading and learning more about ancient Egypt. During this time, I discovered inside myself a buried love of archaeology." She paused and popped another grape into her mouth.

Reluctantly, Cleo leaned forward and took a cracker with a piece of cheese off the tray. She lifted it to her mouth and took a timid bite. Crumbs fell in her lap, and Cleo quickly brushed them onto the floor. She ignored the horrified look Nefera shot her.

Cleo's mother went on, her eyes becoming more alive the more she talked, "During that time, I began to wonder what my life might have been like if I had been born into the working class, rather than into royal privilege. What trade might I have gone into? Is it possible I would have been one of the treasure hunters—the ones we call archaeologists—who believe it is a privilege to spend every day digging up treasures and artifacts from the past?"

Nefera arched an eyebrow. "The *privilege* of digging? In the *dirt*? Wouldn't you rather have the privilege of admiring these priceless artifacts from the comforts of your own palace?"

"That is one nice way to enjoy relics," the girls' mother said. "In fact, it's the only way I knew. And for a long time, while I was hidden away alone, I definitely missed all the comforts of the world I had grown accustomed to. But the longer I was separated from the lush lifestyle I had been living, I discovered I had an urge to learn and to contribute to the world." She stopped and laughed—that same warm belly laugh Cleo could remember from years before—then went on, "Contribute in a bigger way than just hosting amazing parties."

"But amazing parties are important!" Nefera argued.

"Of course parties are fun and important in their own way," their mother agreed. "But there are many other things that are even more important. Learning from history, caring for others, contributing to society..."

Cleo suddenly thought of the glamorous welcome-home ball she and her father and sister had been planning for that weekend. Would her mother truly enjoy it? And Cleo couldn't help but wonder: Did her mother have anything to *wear* to a ball?

"Well," Cleo's mother continued. "When, finally, it was safe for me to come out of hiding and rejoin the rest of you, I set out on my journey to the Boo World. But along the way, I came upon a team of archaeologists who needed some help.

Part of their team hadn't made it to the site, and they offered me the chance to join their crew. I missed you all very much, but in a life as long as ours is, a few weeks seemed such a small sacrifice. If I joined their dig, I would finally have a chance to contribute to society in a more important way."

"So what happened?" Cleo asked, totally captivated by her mother's story. "Why has it been years, rather than weeks, since we last saw you?"

Her mother smiled sadly. "Everything was going as expected on the dig. We found many interesting treasures in the tomb we had uncovered. While I was at the dig site, I learned far more in a few weeks than I had in all the books I read while I was in hiding. I also became very self-sufficient and learned that there are far worse things in the world than getting your hands dirty during a day's work."

"I beg to differ," muttered Nefera.

"Just as we were about to wrap up our project," Dedyet continued, ignoring Nefera's comment, "tragedy struck. The small mouth of the tomb we were inside caved in, and the entire crew—including me—was trapped inside. It wasn't until last week that we were discovered and freed." She smiled at her family, then said with a flourish, "And now, I am finally home. And the next era of our lives can begin!"

Written Record of Cleo de Nile

Oh my Ra, Mother's arrival was quite a shock.

Father, Nefera, and I had been expecting the mother we remembered from so many years ago....And that certainly isn't what we got!

I am so confused. My mom seems very happy, but she's so different. I can't help but wonder...is there _anything_ we have in common anymore? She and I have been living totally different lives all these decades. She talks about things like reading and studying, and while I do those things too (a ghoul has to keep up her grades!), I also love to shop and go to parties and fang out with my friends. I don't think my mom enjoys those types of things anymore. What will she think of me when she realizes I am so different from her?

Not only does she act different, Mom also looks totally different. She no longer seems to care about fashion—she was wearing jeans and a plain shirt! I had been so excited to show her my closet—it's filled with the latest pieces from the Boo York runways—but I think maybe she doesn't care about clothes anymore.

How did this happen? And _why_ did this happen?

Mother donated all her jewels to a museum to say thank you after she and the other archaeologists were freed from the tomb. That was nice of her to do, but what jewels will she wear now?

I can't imagine what my ghoulfriends are going to say when they meet my mother.... I've been promising them royalty and glamour and elegance. The mummy who resurfaced is anything but.

Oh. My. Ra. What am I going to do?

Cleo

CHAPTER FOUR

Y ou've been really quiet today, Cleo," Draculaura said, nudging her ghoulfriend and captain during fearleading practice the next afternoon. The ghouls of the fearleading squad had stopped to take a water break and go over the steps one more time. Hard as she tried, Draculaura just couldn't seem to get the end of the routine down. Cleo was hoping a short break might help her ghoulfriend refocus on the steps, and then they could finally nail the piece.

"Have I?" Cleo said, tossing her hair over her shoulder. She waved at Deuce, who was playing Casketball with some of his friends on the other side of the Monster High gym. With all the excitement over her mother's arrival and preparations for her welcome-home ball, Cleo hadn't gotten to speak to him all day. "I guess I'm just worried about perfecting our new dance. I'm also really wrapped up in my mother's welcome-home ball. It's going to be a *huge* event, and I want everything to go perfectly. I'm *sure* it will, but there are just so many details to figure out that I'm a little distracted."

"I'm totes excited about it!" Draculaura squealed. "When does your mother arrive? Are you nervous to see her after so much time has passed?"

Cleo gave a dismissive wave. She hadn't told

any of her ghoulfriends yet that her mom had *already* arrived…because she hadn't quite figured out how to tell them that all the memories of her mom had turned out to be very different from the woman who was now living in their house. She was hoping that after her mother had a day or two to settle in, she might start to resemble the mother Cleo had promised all her friends. "She actually arrived last night," Cleo said, forcing a smile. "She's…here!"

"Is she everything you remembered and more?" Frankie asked eagerly, joining their conversation.

"Did she bring a huge trunk full of glamorous clothes with her from Egypt?" Draculaura wondered. "I bet Clawdeen will be itching to get her paws on the latest Egyptian fashions!"

"Mother actually hasn't had time to unpack yet," Cleo said quickly. After seeing her mom's jeans the night before, and the casual (and *very* wrinkled) linen outfit she was wearing around the house after breakfast that morning, Cleo had a feeling her mom did *not* have a trunk full of glamorous clothes. She had a terrible feeling her mother had a trunk full of junk.

But by responding to Draculaura's question in the way she had, Cleo wasn't *lying* to her friends, either—because she didn't know for *sure* what kinds of clothes her mother had brought along with her. Her trunk was, in fact, still packed. And Cleo was sure that with time, her mother would adjust back to the de Nile way of life—all luxury and glamour and fashion. Maybe there were a few fashion gems hidden somewhere in her luggage. If not, Cleo would be more than happy to lend her mother a few pieces from her own wardrobe.

Cleo was just as evasive in answering Frankie. "Oh, it's been years since we last saw her, so of *course* she's changed a bit." Cleo didn't add that

56

by "changed a bit" she actually meant "changed completely." "Most ghouls tend to change at least somewhat with time—I mean, can you imagine if we were still wearing last year's fashions? It would be a monstrous tragedy."

"So where has she been all these years?" asked Draculaura. The little vampire began stretching, which reminded Cleo it was time for the squad to get back to practice. They needed to move things along so Cleo could get home and carry on with preparations for the ball. Cleo hoped that once the time came to tell her mother about the ball, Dedyet de Nile would remember how great her old life was. But before they could tell her about the ball, they had to make sure all the preparations were ready. There was still so much to do!

While the ghouls on the squad lined up to take their new routine from the top, Cleo said proudly, "My mother has been on a very important archaeological dig! She risked her life to assist a team of researchers and archaeologists."

Frankie, Draculaura, and the other girls on the fearleading squad exchanged a surprised look.

"Digging for treasure, relics, and important artifacts from Egyptian history is very glamorous," Cleo added, a bit defensively. "She was assisting a team of scientists and learning about our Egyptian scaritage and the importance of history to our future."

"Was—was she actually…" Draculaura began timidly. "…doing the *digging*?"

Cleo rolled her eyes. "Of course she was actually doing the digging." Before anyone could press her for more details, Cleo started the music and counted off. "Now let's get back to work."

As the ghouls ran through the routine again, Cleo tried to lose herself in the music. She wasn't sure why she wasn't telling her best ghoulfriends more about her mother. Cleo was actually very proud of who her mother had become...but there was still something so unfamiliar about her that she wasn't quite sure how to deal with all the changes.

In fact, all day she had been just the teensiest bit worried about the welcome-home ball. After seeing her mother prepare her own snack in the mansion's kitchen and walk around in a pair of falling-apart slippers, Cleo wasn't so sure the elaborate party they had been planning was even appropriate anymore. She worried that her mother might find all the extravagance over-the-top. And there was still the burning question of what she would actually *wear* to the ball.

But by the time they reached the end of rehearsal, Cleo had managed to put her worries about the ball out of her mind. Because she had more immediate problems—specifically, Draculaura *still* couldn't get the steps for their new routine down, no matter how many times they went over it.

"I'm so sorry, Cleo," Draculaura said with a sad, little shrug. "I don't know why I'm having so much trouble with this new routine."

Cleo shook her head. "Stop apologizing," she said, gently scolding her ghoulfriend. One of the things that irritated Cleo was hearing people apologize for things they had no need to apologize for. Draculaura was *trying*—so there was no reason she should be sorry for her efforts. It wasn't her fault. It's not as if she was being lazy or getting distracted. She was putting in her best effort, and still, the routine just wasn't working. Clearly, something wasn't clicking for Draculaura. "Why don't I stay after practice with you, and we can go over the whole thing again? Maybe if we break it down and rehearse the routine piece by piece, it will stick."

"Really?" Draculaura asked hopefully as the rest of the squad filed out of the Monster High gym. "But you must have so many other things to do! Your mother just came home, so you must be eager to spend time with her. Don't you remember how, when we went to my father's wedding in Transylvania, all I wanted to do was spend time with him after being away from him for many months? And there are all the preparations for the ball you need to complete before this weekend...." She trailed off, waiting for Cleo to take back her offer to stick around and help. "Don't you have a coffin-load of homework?"

But Cleo simply shrugged and said, "If you nail this routine, it's a good thing for the whole fearleading squad. I'm your captain—and your ghoulfriend—so I'm going to help until you get it. Now let's get to work and see if we can figure it out before they lock the school gates for the night."

"Thanks, Cleo," Draculaura said, grinning. "I really appreciate it."

Cleo turned on the music and began to count off. "Don't mention it," she said, flashing a smile back at her ghoulfriend.

Written Record of Cleo de Nile

While I was spending a little extra time helping Draculaura get our fearleading squad routine down, I had the most golden idea. Much like Draculaura and our new dance, Mother's elegance and fashion sense obviously just need a little extra practice. With time—and help from an expert—I'm sure she can dig up her old self. My old mother is in there . . . she just needs to be uncovered. And since I have had years to perfect being a de Nile, who better to help her than ME?

If anyone has mastered the art of being royal, it is I (okay, and maybe Nefera—but she's so unpleasant about her status that she gives royalty a bad name!). Maybe I can help Mom remember what it is to be part of this family by fixing her up so she can recall what it feels like to be glamorous and important.

Perhaps part of the reason Mother is so...well...messy is that she has forgotten how to put herself back together. She's had so many years living in that creepy, old tomb—in the dark! Oh my Ra!—that she hasn't had to worry about makeup or fashion or skin care.

Though I know the welcome-home ball will be totally fangtastic, I think there's something even more important I can do for Mother to truly welcome her home and whisk her back to the life to which she was once accustomed: It's time for a creeperific mom makeover!

Cleo

CHAPTER FIVE

By the time Cleo left Monster High after an hour of extra practice with Draculaura, she was buzzing with excitement. She couldn't believe she hadn't thought of giving her mother a makeover sooner! After all, Dedyet de Nile had practically been *buried* for years, so she probably desperately needed someone to advise her on how fashion and makeup and hairstyles had evolved while she'd been under wraps on her dig.

Surely Cleo's mother hadn't made a conscious *choice* to wear the jeans and linen outfit and the awful hairstyle she had arrived in. She just didn't know any better! Cleo couldn't wait to restore her mother to her former luster—just like one of the antiques in the de Nile palace! If the two of them worked hard, her mom could be back to her old self before the welcome-home ball, and no one would ever have to see the less-than-glamorous relic Cleo's mother had become during her time away.

Cleo couldn't *wait* to help fix all her mom's problems!

But as she rushed across the Monster High lawn to get home to her mother, Cleo spotted Clawdeen Wolf hustling out of one of the side doors of the school. Clawdeen looked monstrously stressed. "Clawdeen," Cleo called out to her fashionable ghoulfriend. "I've been looking for you for days. You've missed lunch three times now, which means you've missed my absolutely *golden* news."

Clawdeen took a deep breath. "I've had a lot going on the last few days," she said. "Family stuff."

"I have exciting family news too," Cleo said, momentarily oblivious to Clawdeen's stressed-out expression. "My mother has returned home after a very extended absence, and my family will be having a ball to welcome her home this weekend. You are, of course, invited."

"That's clawesome, Cleo," Clawdeen said a bit distractedly. "I can't wait to meet her."

Cleo tilted her head to one side. Something was off about her ghoulfriend, but she wasn't sure what. "Aren't you going to ask me if you can design my dress for the event?"

Clawdeen sighed. "Does that mean you *want* me to design your dress for the ball?"

"I would be willing to give you the honor," Cleo replied with a grin.

"You know I'd love to—" Clawdeen began.

"Then it's settled," Cleo broke in. "I'd like something gold, perhaps with some hints of green—"

Clawdeen shook her head. "You didn't let me finish. I was going to say that I'd love to help, but I'm totally swamped with a project for my sister right now. Clawdia has a big book-launch party she's going to, and I promised I'd make her something creeperific to wear. I've been working on designing her dress for a week, but I just can't find the right fabric in my supplies or at the fabric store. Between the dress problem and my soccer tournament last weekend and family visiting from out of town this week and a Clawculus exam tomorrow, I just don't think I'll have time to design something that will live up to your standards right now. I'm so sorry, Cleo, but I'm sure you can find something creeperific at Neiman Monstrous."

"You want me to buy a dress *off the rack*? Not going to happen," Cleo said, shuddering. Unwilling to take no for an answer, Cleo said, "Can I see the design for Clawdia's dress?"

Clawdeen shifted her things in her arms and pulled out a sketchbook. She opened it to the back pages and showed Cleo the design-in-progress. "I was hoping to find a shimmery fabric, but the problem is, I need something that will also drape well. Clawdia looks great in navy, but I was also considering gold." Clawdeen paused for a moment to grin at Cleo. "You can never go wrong with gold, right?"

"Never," Cleo agreed. She studied Clawdeen's sketch for another moment, then said, "I think I might have something you could use! Why don't you come over to my house and take a look in my closet? I have a dress I wore last year that might work perfectly for this. It's totally last-season, so I'll never wear it again. You're welcome to repurpose the fabric for your design if it would work."

"I've looked everywhere, and I think the fabric I need doesn't exist... but it's worth a shot!" Clawdeen said.

"You haven't looked everywhere until you've looked in *my* closet," Cleo replied, linking her arm through Clawdeen's.

✤   ✤   ✤

When the two ghouls arrived at the de Nile palace, Cleo quickly led Clawdeen straight upstairs. They didn't stop to ask the servants to prepare them a snack, instead rushing through the palace hallways and making their way directly to Cleo's room.

As Clawdeen pawed through Cleo's closet full of old dresses, she said, "Is your mother home now? I'd love to meet her if she is. Maybe—if I can get Clawdia's dress done in time—I could try to design something clawesome for both of you to wear to the event. I'd love to meet her and see what would best suit her."

"Oh," Cleo said, biting her lip. "She's, um…not home right now. She's at the salon, getting a deep condition. See, she's been on this archaeological dig, and the tomb air really dried out her hair." The lie just slipped out. Of course Cleo was excited to introduce her mother to her Monster High ghoulfriends, but she really wanted to wait until she'd had a chance to make her over first. The big reveal would have so much more impact if she were restored to her former luster!

Eager to change the subject, Cleo grabbed the

dress she had been thinking of off the hanger. "Here it is," she said to Clawdeen. "Don't you think this material would be perfect for Clawdia's dress?"

Clawdeen rubbed the fabric between her thumb and forefinger. The soft, shimmery satin was *exactly* what she had been searching for. "Are you sure about this, Cleo? This dress is beautiful, and it would be ruined if I cut it up to make Clawdia's dress!"

Cleo waved her hand dismissively. "I'm absolutely positive. This dress *is* beautiful, but I just don't see myself wearing it ever again. Putting the fabric to good use on one of your creeperific designs is *much* better than letting it get dusty inside my closet. If you can use the fabric, it's yours." As she led Clawdeen back to the front door of the palace, Cleo added, "And if you need a model to try it on for you before you send it to Clawdia, you know where to find me. I always like to be the first to wear new fashions, you know."

"Oh, I know," Clawdeen said with a laugh. "Thanks again, Cleo."

Moments after she had closed the door behind her ghoulfriend, Cleo heard her mother's voice from inside the study. "Is that you, Cleo, dear?"

Cleo made her way to the study, where she found her mom hunched over a pile of old-looking books. Cleo's mother looked up from the desk, her hair and glasses askew. "Hi, Mom," Cleo said. "How was your day?"

"Good, good. Your father has been helping me catalog some of our antiques," her mother said. "We've been having so much fun digging through some of our oldest treasures. We have decided to send a few important pieces to a museum in Boo York—they're extremely grateful for the loan."

Cleo's mother pushed her glasses up, then tilted her head to the side. "Did I hear someone else's voice in the entryway? That wasn't one of your Monster High ghoulfriends, was it?"

"Actually, it was," Cleo said. "Clawdeen Wolf is a fashion designer. I'm helping her with a piece she's making for her sister."

"Why didn't you introduce me?" her mother asked. "I would love to meet some of your friends from school."

"About that," Cleo said, feeling just the slightest bit nervous all of a sudden. "I was thinking— don't you want to look your best before you meet my ghoulfriends?"

Her mother frowned. "What do you mean?"

"I just mean..." Cleo began, eager to see her mother's reaction to the makeover idea. "Well, I've had an idea—what do you think about my giving you a makeover?"

"A makeover?" Cleo's mother repeated, frowning even more deeply.

"Yes!" Cleo said, clapping her hands excitedly. "I'll get an appointment at my favorite salon for you to get your hair done—highlights, lowlights, a fresh cut, the works. Then we can set up a meeting with my stylist to put your wardrobe back in order. And, of course, we should stop at the spa for skin treatments and mani-pedis. We can even invite Nefera, if you insist. Afterward, I'll help you do your makeup, and we can get rid of some of your dusty, old dig wardrobe. Out with the old, in with the new!"

Dedyet de Nile raked one unmanicured hand through her hair. "I see."

Cleo's smile faded. "You see? See what?"

"Are you embarrassed to introduce me to your ghoulfriends, Cleo?" her mother asked. "Is that what you're saying?"

"No!" Cleo insisted. "I just thought you might *want* to fix yourself up before you meet every-one. You never get a second chance for a first impression. And if your first impression here in the Boo World is...well, *this*..." She gestured to her mother's outfit and hair and makeup-free face.

Cleo's mother nodded seriously. "It's not the impression I ought to be making. Is that what you think?"

"Exactly," Cleo said, relieved that her mother agreed. "But we'll get you fixed up in no time. I can't wait to help unwrap your true beauty!"

"So...you would be happy to help me change who I've become?" Cleo's mom asked.

"Of course! We'll restore you back to your most beautiful self in no time."

Cleo's mother looked at her daughter for a long moment. When she finally spoke again, her voice was soft but firm. "I'm sorry you feel this way, Cleo. But I'm happy with who I am."

"You mean you're happy with these clothes and this hairstyle?" Cleo asked, her eyes wide with disbelief.

Her mom chuckled as she looked down at her plain pants and wrinkled shirt. "I guess I am happy with my clothes. And my hair too, now that you mention it. I can see how this might be hard for you to digest at first, but those things don't matter very much to me anymore. Can you understand that?"

Even though what her mother was telling her was somewhat shocking to hear, Cleo realized that she was totally fine with it. "Of course I can understand that," she said honestly. "I didn't mean to make you think I don't like you as you are. I really thought maybe you just needed... some *help* getting back to the way you used to be.

But if you're happy, then I'm happy. I really am just glad you're back."

Cleo's mother's face broke into a beautiful smile. "Thank you for understanding, Cleo. I am so glad I'm back too." She reached out and touched her daughter's cheek. "You are very glamorous, and that's wonderful because it makes you happy. I know I am not very glamorous anymore, but I feel good about myself. As long as we are both happy with ourselves, that's all that really matters, right?"

Cleo knew her mother was right. And for the first time since she had returned home, she felt as if her mom was truly *back*.

Written Record of Cleo de Nile

It's not often that this happens, but I was totally wrong about something! I honestly thought Mother would love digging herself out of her dusty, old archaeologist life with a glamorous, creeperific makeover... but as it turns out, my mom is very happy with her new look. She no longer has any interest in going to the spa; she likes her hair the way it is now because she doesn't have to spend as much time each morning getting ready; and she feels most comfortable in worn jeans. Mom asked me if I could understand that, and you know what? I totally can. It's not a look I plan to go for anytime soon, but if she's happy with herself, then that's all that really matters.

Once the makeover was off the table, Mother and I still had a fangtastic night together. She suggested we both put on our favorite pajamas (I went for elegant pajamas, and she went for comfort), then cuddle up on the sofa together, watching boo-vies and eating popcorn, just like we used to do when I was a young ghoul. We watched When Hairy Met Skully and

Five Hauntings and a Wedding. Mom and I might not share the same fashion sense anymore, but we definitely still have the same taste in boo-vies! We both still love those classic romantic comedies.

Tonight Mother also told me a bunch of stories about some of the other monsters that she met and became friends with on the dig. Hearing her speak about her crew—and the ways they looked out for and encouraged one another while they were trapped in the tomb—helped me see how warm and caring Mother is. She even admitted to me that though she'd missed us terribly in the time she was away, if she had the chance to do everything over again, she would still agree to help the crew of researchers. She truly believes that if they hadn't all been trapped in there together, they might not have survived. The members of the group relied on one another for support, encouragement, and friendship during their ordeal, and she would never want to abandon them in their time of need.

My mom is a wonderful person, and I'm so proud of her. But she is also very different from the woman our family parted with years ago. I wish there were some way I could have my old mom on the outside with this same new mom on the inside. Not because I'm embarrassed of her or anything like that. I just miss knowing that we look <u>exactly alike</u>. It used to make me feel so good when I was a ghoul and other monsters would see us and make a fuss over how much we looked alike.

I loved being her mini-me. Now I'm not sure anyone would see the resemblance anymore, and that does make me a little sad. But it's all worth it having her back home!

Cleo

CHAPTER SIX

leo, how many times must I tell you?" Nefera said in a weary voice. "The golden wall hangings clash with the silver in the centerpieces. How horrified will Mother be if we have *clashing* accessories at her welcome-home ball?!"

Cleo didn't waste her breath telling Nefera that their mother probably wouldn't care one little bit if the accessories at the party clashed. After the laid-back evening she and her mom had spent together the previous night—and the long talk they'd had about her mom's new look and new outlook on life—Cleo had a suspicion their mother probably wouldn't even *notice* the décor at the ball. Even still, she and her sister had been arguing over the final details for the welcome-home party all afternoon.

Everything was coming together beautifully, and nearly all plans were in place, but Cleo felt as if there was still something off about the gala they were planning. She decided to share her concerns with her sister, with the hope that they could work through the problem together. "Nefera," Cleo said, pushing aside the centerpiece sample and images of wall-hanging options. "I've been a little worried about surprising Mom with this party. Do you think we should tell her about the ball?"

Nefera gave her sister an irritated look. "This

is a welcome-home gala that is meant to be a surprise," she said. "If we tell Mother we're planning a party in her honor, she will absolutely insist on being a part of the preparations. And it's not fair to the guest of honor to expect her to help plan her own welcome-home celebration."

"I'm not sure that's true," Cleo said.

"Seriously, Cleo?" Nefera said. "How tacky to suggest that someone be involved in planning their own celebration. It's simply not done."

"Not that," Cleo said. "I mean, I'm not sure it's true that Mother will insist on being a part of the planning. In case you haven't noticed, Mother doesn't really seem like the type to concern herself with the details of a royal ball anymore."

Nefera waved her hand in the air. "Nonsense."

"Think about it," Cleo urged. "Do you really think our mom is the kind of monster who will enjoy this kind of attention now? She has changed a lot since we lived together in Egypt. Perhaps something a little more low-key would be better?"

Cleo wasn't sure what she meant by *low-key*, exactly—de Niles didn't really *do* low-key—but she figured it was worth having a conversation about.

"Cleo, darling," Nefera said in a patronizing voice, "once a de Nile, always a de Nile. Mother will love it. This ball is just the thing to help her remember the best parts of our family and get herself back into our way of life." Nefera stood up and made her way to the door of the ballroom. "I'm going to work with Father on the rest of the details for this weekend. You don't seem to have your head in the right place for this."

Cleo watched her go. She wondered if Nefera was right. Just because her mother was no longer glamorous on the outside, did that mean her taste in parties had changed as well? Cleo wasn't sure, but she had this feeling that an elegant ball was a terrible idea. Surely it was important that they try to make their mother's welcome-home celebration an event that actually made her feel welcome. If they carried on with their original plan to hold an evening of luxury and glamour in full de Nile style, it might make their mother feel as if she didn't belong to the family anymore.

As she headed out of the ballroom, Cleo wondered if the best way to make her mother feel welcome was not with a showy ball—but by taking the time to get to know her all over again, as the person she was today. She found her mother reading in the study and plunked down in the chair beside her.

"Hi," Cleo said. "What are you reading?"

Her mother looked up with a smile, then pushed her glasses up on top of her head. "An article about a dig in northern Egypt. It's very interesting."

"Could I read it when you're done?" Cleo asked. "I'd love to know more about what it's like on an archaeological dig."

Cleo's mother nodded and smiled. "Of course. I would very much like to share this part of my life with you."

"Mom," Cleo said, tucking her legs up under herself to get comfortable. "Want to fang out again tonight? Catch up on stuff? You can tell me more about the dig; I can tell you stories about Monster High?"

"I'd love that," her mother exclaimed.

Cleo beamed. "Should I make reservations at Appleboos?" She brightened. "Or we could go shopping? The Maul is absolutely golden—we could look for a few new things for both of us?"

Her mother reached out and squeezed Cleo's

hand. "If that's what you want to do, I'd be happy to do that with you. But to be honest, I would rather just spend the evening here at home, simply enjoying each other's company."

"Don't you miss eating out? Or shopping? Even for the kind of stuff you like now?" Cleo asked, honestly curious. If she had been trapped in a tomb for years, Cleo was certain she'd be eager to eat out at a restaurant or buy some new clothes.

"Not really," her mother said, shrugging. "What I missed most when I was gone was the three of you. Nothing would make me happier than spending the evening with you learning about your ghoulfriends and your activities at Monster High." She leaned in closer and whispered, "And are there any *boys* I should know about? You avoided that question the other night."

Cleo laughed. She had a feeling her mother

was going to *love* laid-back Deuce. "Oh my Ra, there's *so much* for us to get caught up on." Then Cleo settled in for a long chat, thrilled that she had the opportunity to get to know her mother all over again.

Written Record of Cleo de Nile

It's clear to me now that we never needed to make over my mom…but we absolutely do need to make over the plan for her welcome-home party. I have always prided myself on planning perfect parties. Surely I can come up with some way to twist this old-fashioned royal ball into something that feels totally de Nile but is also perfectly suited to my dig-in-the-dirt, down-to-earth mother.

I just know that trying to force Mom into the kind of party that no longer suits who she has become is NOT the right way to welcome her home to us.

A few ideas I've come up with:

- Deuce's pool-party suggestion (But our wrappings will get very wet, which is never ideal)
- A backyard barbecue (Too common?)
- Perhaps we turn this into a smaller dinner party with only our closest friends (Let's be honest—this idea will disappoint everyone who isn't invited. How does one limit the guest list for a de Nile party? It simply isn't done.)

Ugh. That's all I've got. I think I'm going to have to enlist the help of my ghoulfriends to figure this one out. But first, I'll have to tell them what Mother is really like. . . . This will be interesting. I know everyone at Monster High has very high expectations for the de Nile family—what will my ghoulfriends say when they realize my mother is so different from the rest of us?

Cleo

CHAPTER SEVEN

Do you have a minute, Cleo?" Lagoona Blue asked, sliding into the empty seat beside Cleo the next morning.

"Of course," Cleo said, glancing up from the magazine she had been reading. While she was waiting for math class to start, Cleo had been reading through a bunch of articles about archaeological digs. Her mother had recommended a few pieces she could read to learn more about the topic, and Cleo was really enjoying herself. She could see why her mom had been so interested in joining a team of researchers. "What's up, Lagoona?"

Lagoona rested her chin on her hand and sighed. "It's about Gil."

Cleo frowned. Lagoona Blue and Gil Webber were one of the most fintastic couples at Monster High. "Is everything okay?"

"Not really," Lagoona said sadly. "I was hoping to get your advice about some issues I'm having with his parents. I have a feeling you'll understand."

"Ah," Cleo said, nodding. "Parent issues. I totally get it." Cleo had spent much of the past year defending her relationship with Deuce to her father. Cleo's dad believed that Deuce wasn't good enough for Cleo—he was always suggesting more appropriate matches—but Cleo knew that wasn't the case at all. Deuce was *different* from the de Niles, but no less amazing.

"His parents can't accept me for who I am," Lagoona said sadly. "They can't seem to get over the fact that I'm a saltwater ghoul and they're freshwater. They keep telling him that our relationship will never stay afloat once we're out in the real world."

"Do you agree with them?" Cleo asked.

"Crikey, no!" Lagoona exclaimed. "Our relationship is swimming along beautifully."

"Then that's what really matters," Cleo said firmly. "You and Gil are very different monsters; that's part of what makes your relationship so special. You offer each other a glimpse into a different kind of world than the ones you are most familiar with."

Lagoona nodded. "Yeah, you're right, Cleo. I guess part of the reason we have so much fun together is that we did grow up in very different worlds. It's fun getting to know about a different way of life."

Cleo nodded. "In time, hopefully, his parents will begin to realize that too. Sometimes it can take a while—but eventually, I'm sure, they'll begin to see that even though you come from very different worlds, it doesn't mean you don't belong together." As she said it, Cleo realized what she was saying also applied to herself and her mother. They came from different worlds, but that didn't mean they had to feel any less connected to each other.

Lagoona nodded enthusiastically. "You're so right, Cleo. I knew you'd get it. I guess you and Deuce have to deal with a similar situation."

"We do," Cleo said. Then she admitted, "And the same can be said of my mother."

"Your mother?" Lagoona asked. "What do you mean?"

Cleo still hadn't told any of her ghoulfriends about how much her mother had changed. But she knew that the longer she put it off, the more it would seem that she was embarrassed or ashamed about who her mother had become. And if there was one thing she had learned at Monster High, it was that all monsters were unique and special—no matter how different from her they were. Cleo rushed to tell Lagoona all about her mother before class started. When she had finished confessing everything, she said, "I'm a little nervous to tell the other ghouls about her."

Lagoona looked confused. "Why?"

"Because I've been bragging about how glamorous and elegant she is—and she's anything but."

"Does that mean she's any less fangulous?" Lagoona asked.

"Not at all!" Cleo said quickly. "She's wonderful and kind and caring, and I am so proud to have a mom like her.... It's just that she's fangu-lous in a very different way than I was expecting. I don't want the other ghouls to be disappointed that she's not more like me. The world has high expectations for the de Nile family!"

"Oh, Cleo." Lagoona laughed. "You don't have to worry about *that*. We'll adore her no matter what!"

Though Cleo already knew that would be the case, it was definitely nice to hear someone else say it aloud. "Thanks, Lagoona." Just as class started, she leaned over and whispered, "And I hope everything works out with you and Gil."

❖   ❖   ❖

That day at lunch, Cleo finally had a full table to rule over. She sat at the head of the table and declared, "I have an announcement."

While she waited for everyone to focus on her and her alone, Cleo looked around the table at the assortment of best friends she had collected in her time at Monster High: Deuce, Frankie, Lagoona, Draculaura, Clawdeen. They were all very different types of relics from an assortment of scaritages and eras, but they were all still golden in their own special way. None of them were royal or even as glamorous as Cleo, but that didn't make any of them any less special. Her mother was the perfect new addition to Cleo's collection of loved ones. She couldn't wait to put her on display!

"I have a problem," Cleo said bluntly, addressing the table. "And I need your help."

There was a chorus of agreement from everyone at the table—everyone was ready to help.

Cleo went on to tell her friends all about her mother—withholding nothing. Surprisingly, it seemed her friends were even *more* excited to meet her mom now.

Deuce pumped his fist in the air. "This is totally

clawesome!" He whooped. "Are you telling me there's actually a chill de Nile in the house now? This could be seriously good for me."

Cleo laughed. "Yes, Deuce, I think my mom is going to love you." Then she added, "Now, while all this news about my mother is good, I'm afraid there's some bad news too. I don't think a glamorous ball is the best way to welcome her home. I want to adjust the party so it's an event that will allow Mother to be herself. I don't want her to feel she has to change who she is to fit into our family, and I'm afraid throwing a ball for her will do just that."

"No ball?" Deuce said, his smile widening. "Does this mean no suit? This just keeps getting better."

Cleo looked around the table at her friends. "As we all know, I know a thing or two about planning glamorous parties. But low-key parties are a little out of my area of expertise, so I was hoping you would help me." She grinned at her ghoulfriends, and they smiled back at her.

"What can we do to help?" Lagoona asked.

"Well, Lagoona, you did such a creeperific job planning the wrap party after the dance recital last scaremester," Cleo replied, tapping her manicured nails on the table, "I was wondering what ideas you might have for music. And, Clawdeen, that party you threw after your fashion show a few months ago had the most epic decorations. Would you have any ideas for my party?"

The ghouls all began talking at once. Before long, they had a long list of clawesome party ideas. Cleo looked around the table at the excited faces of her friends and felt a surge of happiness. She was one lucky ghoul, and she knew it.

Written Record of Cleo de Nile

Everything has come together monstrously well! Even though Nefera is totally coming unwrapped about our change in plans, I couldn't be happier. With a ton of help from my ghoulfriends, we came up with the best theme idea for Mother's welcome-home bash: a Come As You Are party!

Tonight, in true Monster High style, the de Niles are holding a gala that's all about celebrating WHO YOU ARE, in freaky fabulous style!

Though I expected Father to cringe at the idea of un-glamming the party, he actually seemed relieved when I suggested it. He too was worried about making Mother feel unwelcome. Usually, Father says it's his way or no way at all, so I was surprised he was willing to compromise on this ball. Perhaps he is finally realizing that loving someone who is very different from yourself can open up your world to some exciting new possibilities. I can see that my mom is softening my stiff and stern father already, and she's been home for only a few days!

I think Mother's arrival is really going to shake things up at the de Nile palace—I can't wait to see what kinds of changes will come about over the next few years with her around again. I've often thought Father needed to step outside the comforts of his tomb more often and take a look around to see how much has changed in the world over the past few centuries!

I can't wait to see the look on Mother's face when she sees the party we've put together in her honor. I just hope she realizes how different this party is because of her. This event isn't just a chance to celebrate her homecoming—it's also a chance for us to show her that we're willing to adapt our lifestyle and traditions to suit all the de Niles (unfashionable jeans and all!).

Cleo

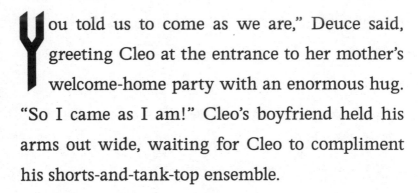

CHAPTER EIGHT

You told us to come as we are," Deuce said, greeting Cleo at the entrance to her mother's welcome-home party with an enormous hug. "So I came as I am!" Cleo's boyfriend held his arms out wide, waiting for Cleo to compliment his shorts-and-tank-top ensemble.

"Really, Deuce?" Cleo asked. She glanced down at her own gown. To celebrate the occasion, she had found the gold gown that she had admired on her mother so long ago. The gown had been waiting all these years for Cleo's mother to return for it. But now that it was clear Dedyet de Nile probably would never wear any of her old gowns again, Cleo had happily taken all her favorites for herself. *Someone* ought to wear them, she reasoned! Clawdeen had helped Cleo reinvent the dress just the slightest bit, to make it feel more in line with modern fashion. She looked like an Egyptian treasure. Deuce, on the other hand, looked as if he had just left the gym. Cleo looked at Deuce and sighed. "We don't match at *all*. No one will even know we're together."

Deuce slung his arm around her shoulder. "We *never* match! But *everyone* knows we're together. We complement each other. Opposites attract and all that, right?"

Cleo laughed, even as she tried to look annoyed. "In our case, that's absolutely true." In fairness, Cleo had told those invited to the party that they could dress for fun...and that there was no expectation that they get glammed up, unless that was their thing. Come As You Are meant come as the *monster* you are—a true celebration of what makes you unique!

For Cleo, that meant donning a fangtastic gown and making herself look elegant and glamorous. The same could be said for some of her ghoul-friends—Clawdeen, Frankie, and Draculaura loved a good excuse to look freaky fabulous. But Deuce? Not so much. The same was true of Lagoona and Gil, who had shown up in casual beach attire and flip-flops. Everyone seemed totally comfortable in his or her Come As You Are outfits. It was creeperific to see all the different styles and monsters mingling together at the same party!

Cleo dragged Deuce and her ghoulfriends across the de Niles' backyard so she could introduce everyone to her mother—finally. After a lot of discussion, Nefera and Cleo had agreed to have the welcome-home party outdoors. In their palace ballroom, it would have been absolutely impossible to make the party feel low-key. By having the party outside, they were better able to accommodate some of Nefera's must-haves, as well as Cleo's wish list, and also incorporate some things that would make the party feel extra-special for their mother too.

"Wow, Cleo," Draculaura said, gazing around the yard. "Everything looks totes amazing."

"You didn't tell me there would be water-slides!" Deuce said. He stared across the yard at an enormous fountain, complete with marble slides and bubbling jets. Ramses de Nile had had it flown in from Egypt for the occasion. "Bummer," Deuce said, snapping his fingers. "I forgot my swimsuit."

"Deuce," Cleo said. "That is *not* a water*slide*. It is a water *feature*—a decorative fountain! Its sole purpose is to be admired. It is very elegant, very expensive, and very old."

"I don't care how old it is." Deuce shrugged. He adjusted his shades and grinned. "It still looks like it would be fun to play in."

As Cleo and her friends made their way across the lawn, they passed elaborate ice carvings (Nefera had insisted), a table heaped with very posh Egyptian cuisine (her dad said that even if they were going low-key with the party, there could be no compromise on the food), and also dozens of Cleo's mother's Egyptian relics displayed in beautiful glass boxes all around the garden. Tomorrow morning, most of the relics would be shipped off to museums in Scaris, Londoom, and Boo York—but tonight, Cleo wanted everyone to be surrounded by treasures from her mother's life.

"Mom," Cleo said, stepping forward to get her mother's attention. "I want you to meet some of my best friends from Monster High."

One by one, Cleo introduced everyone to her mother. Cleo's mother greeted each warmly, instantly charming the group with her down-to-earth style and soft, gentle nature. "Isn't she just the best?" Cleo asked her friends, linking arms with her mother. "But admit it: Aren't you all absolutely shocked to see just how different we are?"

"How do you mean?" Cleo's mother asked, furrowing her brow. "I don't think you and I are *that* different, are we?"

Cleo considered this. For the past few days, she had been thinking quite a bit about the things that set her apart from her mother. There were the obvious things: their differences in style and the fact that her mother was happy with a simpler life. Also, their underlying goals in life were very different: Cleo looked forward to a life of royalty and privilege (with plenty of fun and good friends thrown in, of course!), while her mother aimed to help people and make the world a better place. And Cleo couldn't stop thinking about how much she admired her mother's willingness to make sacrifices to help others: her donation of important family relics to museums for the benefit of other monsters, and all the years of her life she had given up to be a part of the archaeological crew on the dig.

Cleo began to explain all this to her friends, but Draculaura cut her off before she could get very far. "Cleo, even though you and your mother look different on the outside, from what I can tell, you do have something very important in common."

"Royal blood?" Cleo guessed.

"No." Draculaura laughed. "That's not what I meant, you silly ghoul. I was talking about your big, warm heart and your eagerness to always help others."

Cleo tilted her head. "I don't understand."

"Remember when my skirt ripped earlier this week?" Frankie cut in. "It would have been an absolute fashion disaster if you hadn't agreed to help me. You risked getting into trouble with Headmistress Bloodgood just so you could help me!"

"And even though you were very busy planning your mother's party," Draculaura added, "you stayed after fearleading squad practice to help me get our routine figured out."

Cleo smiled. Of *course* she'd done those things— what kind of ghoulfriend wouldn't?

"Don't forget about how much you helped me with my sister's dress," Clawdeen chimed in. "You went out of your way to help me find the perfect fabric."

Lagoona leaned up against Gil and said, "And when I needed love advice you knew *exactly* what to say."

"Not to mention this party," Deuce said. "I know how much you were looking forward to the usual all-out de Nile affair—but you went out of your way to make sure your mom felt welcome." He shrugged. "And I feel a whole lot more welcome too. Shorts and skate shoes at the palace? This rocks."

Cleo's mom wrapped her arm around her daughter and beamed. "These stories make me so happy. Nothing could make me prouder than hearing all the ways you've helped your friends in their times of need. And after all the nice things your ghoulfriends have said about you, I certainly *hope* you and I are more alike than you think, dear." Dedyet de Nile gazed out over her party and said, "In the few days we've had to get reacquainted, it seems to me that you have become the kind of ghoul who is always there for your friends—and that you believe in and go after your dreams no matter what other people might think."

"Yeah," Cleo said, smiling. "That's all true."

"Totes!" Draculaura agreed. The other ghouls nodded too.

Deuce mumbled, "Yeah," through a mouthful of shrimp. "What she said. You rock, Cleo."

"So maybe we live our lives a little differently," Cleo's mom said. Then she gestured to her linen pants and simple tank top, and added, "And perhaps we don't *look* or *dress* alike anymore, though unless I am mistaken, that's one of *my* gowns you are wearing. That one was always my favorite, and I must say, it looks absolutely lovely on you—"

Cleo laughed. Before her mom could finish her thought, Cleo hugged her and whispered, "I'm so glad you noticed the gown. And yes, we really are similar in the most important ways."

"That we are. I'm so proud of you, Cleo," her mother said with tears in her eyes. "It's good to be back."

Written Record of Cleo de Nile

Mother's welcome-home party was a _smashing success!_ The music was golden, thanks to Lagoona's great choices, and Clawdeen's suggestions about the decorations helped to create just the right atmosphere. Draculaura and Frankie came up with some great suggestions for the food. Together, my ghoulfriends and I pulled off the perfect party! And all the guests had a creeperific time. All in all, it was a party worthy of the de Nile name, and one that the guest of honor truly enjoyed.

The ghouls and Deuce couldn't stop talking about how amazing my mom is. I can't wait to make up for lost time with her. We have a long list of boo-vies to catch up on; and now that she's met Deuce and all my ghoulfriends, we have so much to talk about! My mom might not be the most glamorous woman I know anymore—she's not even glamorous _at all_ anymore—but it made me feel really good to hear my ghoulfriends say I'm a lot like her. I want to be _even more_ like her. I don't think I will be adopting her style any time soon . . . and that's okay. She's her, and I am me. And I'm happy for _both of us_!

Cleo

S tart your own creeperific diary, just like Cleo! On the following pages, write about your own creepy-cool thoughts, hopes, or screams...whatever you want! These pages are for your eyes only! (Unless you want to share what you write with your ghoulfriends!)

MONSTER HIGH

Cleo

xxx

Monster High

Cleo

x x x

Monster High

Did you ♥ reading Cleo's diary?
Then you will love reading
THE OTHER MONSTER HIGH DIARIES!